For Deb...
Hope ya enjoy. ♡
Keep in touch...

When I Dream of You

By Rosa Sophia

Rosa Sophia

P.S. This is
auto-biographical
fiction.

When I Dream of You

Limitless Publishing, LLC
Kailua, HI 96734
www.limitlesspublishing.com

Formatting: Limitless Publishing

ISBN-13: 978-1502392695
ISBN-10: 1502392690

Dedication

To Florida, the home of my soul.

Chapter 1

Present day, Jupiter, Florida

My mother was drunk in the next room when it happened twelve years ago.

Now I'm sitting in a hotel that could be anywhere. I can hear the ocean lapping against the shore, and the lights of the city look like stars that hang too close to the horizon.

I know I shouldn't be here. Sitting on the firm mattress, my legs bent toward me, I lean against the headboard. I take another drink of whiskey, let the burn sink deep. I feel it in my core, tingling. My breath quickens. I want to be here.

He lifts the comforter and draws me down with him, and I feel as if it's something we've already done. Somewhere, sometime before, he held me this way. And I had to let go.

I can hear his heart beating, my cheek pressed to his chest. I wonder how I ended up here, in the arms of a man I dreamt of before we met. His grip tightens, and I feel soft kisses against my bare shoulder, his stubble scratching my skin. The warmth of his breath is welcome, somehow rejuvenating. Our lips meet and each kiss is exploratory, tender, slow—as if to make sure it's right. I think about the hot tub six floors down. Is the water too searing? Should we get in?

We stop, cuddle, then continue, and I'm too afraid to move. My heart pounds. I start to hear things in my head, familiar voices. Each taunting, jeering. *You stupid slut, what makes you think you're good enough for him?*

I shove them away. He kisses me again, and I invite it. Deep, passionate, frenzied—I've never felt anything like this before. Because I make a point to avoid it.

His hands roam my body, and I respond, wanting more.

Please go away, no, stay!

He presses against me, and I want to welcome him, thrust my hips up to meet his. But suddenly I feel trapped, unable to resist. And his tongue is probing my mouth, and I'm hot, wet between my legs—

Panic. Twelve years ago I was lying on a bed with a broken spring, pinned beneath a man who was laughing at me, shoving himself inside me despite my begging him to stop. He thought it was so funny, my resistance, like the way an adult cackles at a crying child after playing a cruel joke.

Why did you let him do that to me, Mama? Why didn't you stop him?

Stumbling, wasted, she slammed her calloused feet against the faux wood floor and growled, "I *trusted* you!" Brandishing a gnarled finger, she looked at me in disgust, as if—

It was all my fault.

Panic. I'm back in the hotel, and I'm pressing against his chest, trying to pull away from his kisses. The surf licks the sand, warm and wet, and I can hear the syllables as they jump from the sea.

You are worthless. You deserve this. To be humiliated. Scorned. Treated like dirt.

"Please, please no, this is too much for me." I manage to speak, and he stops. Am I talking to him, or the voices? I pull away, my chest aching, my heart sinking. I clutch my stomach. "It hurts."

Something tells me it's not the whiskey; it's the pain I bury, the grief roiling inside me.

I tell him about the rape. How my mother was there. She didn't stop it. Is that love? What is love? I suddenly wish I were six floors down, sinking in the hot tub, nothing but a shell without a soul.

A while later, he asks me if I'm all right, his head on my stomach, his arm around my hip.

I don't know. I don't know if I'm all right.

A year ago I had a vision I was in a hotel room with a man, and we made passionate love for hours. Then he went to war and died, shot in the chest, fallen on a dirt road.

I drag myself off the bed, capping the whiskey, listening to the voices taunt me.

Don't listen. They're wrong.

"I should go," I tell him, but I don't really want to.

He walks me to my car, and I ask him to kiss me again, make it the best I've ever had. And he does.

Driving down the empty roads, I want to turn around and know I shouldn't.

In a hotel room, I realized my fears. Now instead of *him* leaving, it is I who is departing.

A balmy sea breeze tousles the palm trees.

And I drive on, gaze piercing the darkness, thinking of the man I dreamt about before I met him.

Chapter 2

Twelve years ago

The Celtic cross pendant was a gift from my best friend Jenny, and I twirl it between my fingers all day at school.

When I stop by the bathroom in between classes, the tall, willowy Patchett twins are standing in the corner by the paper towel dispenser, giggling with Meghan Chambers. The girls go silent as I step in, and they glare at me as if I don't belong. A lump rises in my throat, and I cast my gaze to the floor.

Those girls hang around *his* crowd; they aren't really friends with him—the monster who raped me last week. I wonder if anyone is *really* his friend, or if they're just using him because he's popular in school and has a lot of connections, or he *says* he does anyway. I'm not sure what is true and what isn't. The only thing I know is that I feel dirty, used, and I hate the part of me between my legs, and I hate my mother because she didn't stop it. But then again, I couldn't cry out, I couldn't call for her. I was too humiliated. *You deserve it*, the voices whisper. I shake my head, cringing, forcing them away. I want to cry. I want to go home, but I don't know where home is.

When I emerge from the stall and wash my hands, I look to the cross for comfort while the girls behind me whisper something and laugh again.

I check myself quickly to make sure I'm okay— shirt straight, pants zipped, nothing embarrassingly out of place. It doesn't matter, they will laugh anyway. But for the rest of the day I'll worry something's showing, something's wrong with me that disappoints them. I still can't figure out why.

Wads of food—soft pretzels, snacks—bounce off my shoulder during lunch. Jenny is out sick, and the only time the kids leave me alone is when she's there, because no one messes with Mayor Bob Tomlin's daughter. No one picked on me when the monster wanted my company. No one would dare throw food at him. But now that he's gotten what he came for, he is gone, and occasionally I see him on the other side of the cafeteria, and I quickly avert my eyes.

I finish my lunch, perched on a seat at the end of an empty table, and watch Adam's snide expression as he leers at me from nearby. A piece of pretzel flies through the air, and lands somewhere in front of my table. Adam saunters over and snatches the pretzel off the ground and says, "I dropped something."

His friends burst into laughter, clutching their guts as Adam goes back to the table and prepares to fire another round.

You'd think I'd be used to it by now.

I tug my backpack across the table and use it as a pillow, folding my arms under my face and resting my head against the cool fabric. I pretend I'm not there. Once I tried to draw a picture of the dreadful feelings that course through me at a time like this, because it was so hard to explain in words. It begins in the center of my chest, a pulsing heaviness that makes it difficult to breathe. Then it spreads across my body like poison, jabbing into my arms and slicing through my fingers. It is misery, a physical reaction that can last anywhere from a few minutes to an entire day. I shuffle my feet, finally resting one over the other, and take a deep breath.

Tears. Hot and salty. They slip unbidden along my cheeks, but I dare not make a sound. I can't let them see me like this.

Under my breath, I repeat the only prayer I know by heart, using the words as a mantra to keep my weeping under control.

"Our Father, who art in Heaven, hallowed be thy name, thy kingdom come, thy will be done in earth as it is in Heaven..."

I clutch the cross so tightly I think it might cut my skin.

***

I always come home late to avoid Mom. I go to the library after school to study or write stories. It's quiet there, peaceful, within walking distance of my bus stop, and I often wonder what would happen if I just stayed there, hid from the librarians at closing time, and slept somewhere in a study room, tucked in a dark corner.

Come find me, I dare you...No, please don't...

I step inside the apartment and carefully shut the door behind me. It is chilly, mid-December, and Mom has the sliding glass doors to the balcony wide open. The breeze reaches across the living room and down the hall, making wind chimes sing in the darkness.

Just because it's dark doesn't mean she's asleep.

Seven-thirty. Mom goes to sleep early most nights, passed out from too many drinks. Most of the time she's out cold by now, but when I walk past her bedroom, I see a wavering form move in the shadows.

"Nina, is that you?"

"Yes, Mom." I leave my backpack on the floor by the front door as I go into the kitchen.

"What are you doing, sweetheart?"

"Making something to eat." I flip on the light switch, and a glaring bright light fills the small space, making me wince.

She joins me a moment later, a thin woman in navy blue pajamas, her short brown hair messy from lying in bed. There are dark circles around her blood-shot eyes, and she leans against the entryway to the kitchen for support, moving back and forth on her gnarled feet as though being pushed to and fro by the breeze.

I don't speak as I gather items for a sandwich—bread, mayonnaise, cheddar cheese, tomato, lettuce, sliced turkey. I feel her watching me.

"What?" I turn, looking at her.

"You're eating now?"

"Yeah. I'm hungry. So what?" I feel it coming. My heartbeat quickens. She will go into her usual diatribe, her breath reeking of liquor.

"It's almost eight o' clock, and you're eating? You'll get fat."

I am so sick of hearing it, I laugh it off. At a hundred and twenty-eight pounds, I am not fat at all, but I can't help but shoot back a clever retort, "Mom, I'm already fat, what does it matter?"

Under the unnatural light, her face contorts in disgust, and she looks almost frightening. She sneers at me. "Look at you. What have you done to yourself?" Her gaze travels up and down my body. "You've gained weight. Why? Look at you."

"Are you serious?"

"Nina, I just don't understand it." She shakes her head, waving her hand in a gesture of disdain, and turns on her heels, nearly stumbling against the plaster wall behind her as she makes her way back to her bedroom.

I move slowly, putting the sandwich together as though I'm building a work of art. Then I stare at it as it sits there on the yellow-and-white plate, the florescent lights above me buzzing.

My appetite is gone. But I eat it anyway.

Then I go in my room and sit on my bed, touching the mattress, running my hands over the blanket. I hear my mother in the next room talking to herself or to the television, I can't tell which.

And I think to myself, *this is where it happened. This is where he raped me.*

Will I ever be able to forget?

Chapter 3

Two weeks ago, Jupiter, Florida

I stand in a sea of people with no room to move. My bare leg brushes against someone's hand. I slip to the side only to collide with a blonde dressed in bright pink. She flashes white teeth and apologizes, her blue eyes sparkling, as she glances at the headband across my forehead that reads *I thought they said RUM.*

I love being around all these people, being part of a race. The energy, the positivity, the competitive urge. It makes me want to grow, shoot for the sky, become a better person.

"And they're off!" The announcer's voice is amplified over the crowd as we begin to move slowly in one direction. For a brief moment, we shift as one flesh, before gaining independence from one another like atoms splitting in an explosion of sweat and excitement.

As we wind around the curve that will lead us along the ocean, I remember last year when I almost vomited after crossing the finish line. Not today.

My feet pound on the pavement and I clear my mind, slipping into a meditative state as I concentrate on my breathing and the alternating pattern of my feet touching the ground as they carry me along.

Snippets of conversations bounce around me.

"Slow at first, then finish strong..."

"Oh, you did? I ran that one too."

"This isn't like the run for the pies, the Thanksgiving run...you know? More intensive..."

I jog past a woman who is running beside a young boy, telling him, "you can do this, don't give up, I know it's your first time, but you can do it." I imagine it's his coach, and I wonder what it's like to not be isolated as a child, to grow up with other kids, with other people encouraging you.

Letting go of thoughts, I clear my mind.

Mom said she thought sports were too much for little children, but I knew the real reason she didn't like them. Evening was her time to drink, and she couldn't drive me to any practice, any function. So I stayed home.

Back to the present, I clear my mind again. I have to concentrate to keep myself from giving up, collapsing by the side of the street. I always want to give up, and the voices encourage it.

Why are you doing this? Such a waste of your time.

"Fuck you," I growl under my breath.

When I Dream of You

A man runs alongside me, glances at me with a peculiar expression, and I hope he didn't think I was talking to him. My cheeks burn, but I can't tell if it's from the heat or my embarrassment.

I jump forward out of my body, my corporeal form tugging me along. A therapist once told me that it was called *dissociation*, said it was a bad thing. But it focuses me; I feel nothing, and I glide along with perfect ease. I can snap back to reality if I choose, but during these races I tend to remain separate, forcing my body through any pain it might encounter all the way to the finish line.

I run for the love of it. I started a couple of years ago, battling depression and weight gain, and now I am a paltry hundred and fifteen pounds, slim and curvaceous, with shoulder-length auburn hair pulled back in a ponytail, perky breasts accentuated by my tank top and sports bra. I'm still not good enough for Mom, who swears I need to lose another couple pounds. Growing up, she'd taught me if your thighs touched when you walked, it meant you were fat.

The voices sound like Mom, and they constantly haunt me. I run from them, keeping a good pace, hoping one day I can leave them behind. I love my mother so much it hurts, but she fights against horrors I can't even begin to imagine. She doesn't know she's beautiful, talented. She worked so hard to protect me, to raise me, but she couldn't stop her demons from escaping their cage.

It was inevitable.

I hear the waves as they break against the sand and look up at the palm trees against a backdrop of light blue sky. Soon I'm on my own, just a crowd of people in front of me and behind me. Until I begin to match my pace with a man around my age, late twenties or early thirties, his brown curls bouncing over the sweat that beads on his forehead.

He's wearing shorts and sneakers, and his muscled arms and chest are bare. For a brief moment, our eyes meet, and I feel my soul snap back into my body. I skip forward as my breath increases its cadence, and I'm unsure if it's his influence that caused it, or my quick pace as I beat a rhythm against the sizzling macadam.

Something about him makes me uncomfortable. Maybe it's the way he's looking at me.

I run ahead to try to escape him, but we keep returning to each other, like polarized magnets drawn inexorably back. There's no defying nature's laws.

We're pacing each other, our steps in sync, and there are only so many times we can glance at each other, pretending we aren't looking, before one of us has to say something.

We swing around the halfway point, passing a group of girls clad in matching shirts. A man walking his dog by the side of the road watches, and the dog barks.

Finally our gazes meet and we acknowledge each other.

"Hey, good luck," he says. "Think you'll beat me?"

"No, I think you'll beat me," I retort, my breath labored.

There's magic, synchronicity, and I feel good running beside him, strangers drawn together somehow by our movements. I think about the finish line. The words *objects in motion stay in motion* flash through my mind. I think about him, but I'm not sure why, and for some reason this feels like the most natural place to be, running with him in the summer heat, the sea breeze caressing our faces.

It's almost as if we're the only ones there.

The ocean of people disappears. And there's nothing left but the sea and the wind as it tosses strands of loosened hair across my face.

When we cross the finish line, there are people cheering, and he and I hit the other side at exactly the same moment. Then we start laughing, and I lean against my knees, huffing. After a moment, I straighten, my hands on my hips.

"I'm Wes, Wesley Ladner," he says.

"Nina Archer. Nice...to meet you."

"Just breathe," he reminds me as we accept our finisher's medals from a grinning middle-aged volunteer wearing a Palm Beach Roadrunners t-shirt. The announcer's voice booms around us, and we walk toward an open patch of grass to relax and stretch. "Are you here with anyone?" he asks.

I'm not sure if he's trying to find out if I'm single, or just being chatty, so I hesitate. "Oh, I just come to these things by myself. I don't really know any other runners."

"Now you do." His smile is so inviting I feel immediately comfortable around him, and I can't help but return his warmth.

He reaches out, then stops, and I'm not sure what he's doing until he touches my forehead, gently brushing the hair out of my face with his fingers. A tremble passes through me and goose bumps rise on my flesh despite the heat.

"Sorry for touching you." He steps back, seeming almost confused, as if the same sensation passed through him. As if something had compelled him to touch a total stranger, and he wasn't sure why.

"No, it's okay."

I try to remember the last time a man touched me. Since I left Dylan two years ago, I haven't dated. Men frighten me. I feel—

Panic.

"Are you sure?"

Our eyes meet. He's my height, and it's hard to escape his gaze. Not that I want to.

"What? Sure about what?" I half-listen to the announcer as he congratulates the top male and top female runners.

"I mean, are you sure it's okay? That was a little weird, I guess, since I just met you. But I can't shake the feeling I've seen you before. Something about your eyes."

"Me too," I agree, perplexed.

"This might be a little presumptuous of me, but would you like to get breakfast with me?" He nods in the direction of the Loggerhead Café on the hill, a squat, yellow building by the beach.

"Yes. Yes, that sounds nice." I could hardly believe the words coming out of my mouth.

When I move to adjust my shirt, tugging it straight against my blue shorts, he takes my hand. At first, I think he's trying to take things too far too quickly, until he gasps and says, "What happened?"

"What do you...?" I glance down at my hands. There's blood on my palms, mingling with my sweat, spreading from small cuts in my soft flesh.

Now I see why my therapist frowned on dissociation.

I'd clenched my fists so tightly my nails had drawn blood.

***

We both take off our race bibs, and I walk with him to his car so he can get a shirt to wear in the restaurant. I'm grateful for this, because his body is a distraction that quickens my pulse as blood rushes between my legs. I've never felt such an instantaneous attraction, and as he lifts his arms and tugs a plain white t-shirt over his head, my gaze darts to the wispy hairs just above the elastic band of his shorts. I glance away fast, not wanting him to catch me.

What is wrong with me?

This is not the voices, but my own self-doubt, my own fear of intimacy rearing up in the depths of my shadowy subconscious. If he knew what was going through my head—

"So what do you do?" he asks as we walk across the parking lot toward the café.

"I work in a bookstore, and I'm a writer."

"Oh?"

I nod. His smile is magnetic.

"I'm a writer too."

"You are?" My eyes widen in surprise. "What kinds of things do you write?"

"Literary fiction. I have something with an agent right now, actually. I think I'm close to getting it published. What do you write?"

"Everything."

He chuckles. "Everything, huh?" Wes opens the door of the café, and a wave of chatter pours out. He ushers me in, and I step forward, not accustomed to having a man hold a door for me.

A bubbly waitress pops out from behind the counter. "Two?"

Wes nods, and the waitress leads us to the back, seating us at a small table by the window across from each other. We order water and coffee to start.

"I'd love to read your writing sometime," Wes says. "What are you working on now?"

"A novel." I glance down at the menu.

"What's it about?"

"I...it's hard to explain." A foolish titter escapes my lips, because I'm so shy that I often laugh nervously when I don't know what else to do.

"What is it, a dirty book or something?"

He winks, and I balk, gasping, my face flushing. "No! It's...it's...I'll just let you read it sometime, okay?"

"Good. I look forward to it."

"What about you, what do you write?"

"Well, the novel my agent has is mainstream fiction, but I'm also working on a romance. I have an MFA in creative writing, and I also took business classes, so I'm trying to combine my creativity with targeting the market so I can actually sell this thing."

"Wow. You have an MFA?" I am impressed, but I have heard how much they cost—which is why I didn't bother with college, remaining happy at my little job at the bookstore, typing away at home in my off hours.

The waitress takes our order, then sashays away. I turn back to Wes, crossing my arms on the table, and add, "You must be buried in debt."

He shakes his head. "Not at all. Everything's paid off."

My eyes widen in shock. "What? How?"

For a moment, he appears hesitant. "My family has a lot of money. I don't even need to work, but I was working for a long time because I got sick of my parents' politics. They don't think I'll be able to sell this book. They'd rather I be in business. They aren't very supportive that way. They live in a completely different universe, and I've always been the black sheep. Sometimes I think someone dropped me off on their doorstep when I was a baby."

"So, you're rich...you just get anything you want?" I cover my mouth, cringing. "Oh God, that sounded so rude. I'm sorry. I don't get out much. I can't remember the last time I sat down and talked to a human being."

Wes laughs and shakes his head. "Don't worry about it. But to answer your question, pretty much, yes. To me it's embarrassing, but I'm sure there are a lot of people who wish they were in my shoes."

"What does your father do?"

"Actually, my mom is the main breadwinner. She's the CEO of Winder Communications Incorporated."

"Oh!" I'd seen the tall, imposing building that housed the main offices in West Palm Beach. "What about your dad?"

"He was a systems analyst until he met my mom. Now he spends most of his time fishing and sailing. How about your parents?"

"I live with my mom right now. I had to move in with her to save money, so we share an apartment in North Palm Beach." I almost add how I'm losing my mind, how I get panic and anxiety attacks, and some days I'm screamed at or berated, and by the next day she'll forget what she said. Instead, I just smile, an expert at faking that little upturn of my lips, knowing the beam won't reach my eyes.

"And *your* dad?"

I grab a piece of paper—the wrapper that held my fork, spoon, and knife in place—and start folding it into a triangle shape, avoiding his eyes. "He's dead. He died in a car accident when I was ten."

"I'm sorry."

"It's okay."

It isn't okay. It's never okay. But this handsome stranger need not know it. Deep down I worry if he knew my dark secrets, he would walk away. The thought saddens me, because it's so rare that I meet someone I really connect with. And for some reason, I feel the electricity flowing between us.

It is almost as if no one else is in the café. At least it feels that way until the waitress clunks our dishes down in front of us and asks if we need ketchup. We both shake our heads, and she steps over to check on the next table.

I wear a watch, but I don't look at the time until the place empties out, and someone comes up to us and says, "Excuse me, we're closing at two today."

Dumbstruck, I glance up at her. "So?"

"So, it's one-thirty."

The race had taken place that morning, and Wes and I had been sitting there talking for hours. He grabs the check and pays, and we walk out into the afternoon sun.

I've already washed my hands in the bathroom, and I look at my palms. The cuts are red and swollen, but they aren't bleeding anymore.

I let Wes hold my hand when he walks me to my car. And even though the sweat stings my wound, the tingle rushing through me when I touch him makes it worth my while.

Chapter 4

I feel my way through the dark hall, guided by the unnatural light flashing against the plaster from my mother's television set. Loud voices—the volume is too high. I know I'll have trouble sleeping.

"Mom." I gently push open her door. She's reclining on her bed, her eyes glued to the screen. "Mom, can you turn that down?"

"Oh, shut up," she sneers, waving her hand in my direction. "You get to do everything you want, and what do I get?"

"Mom, I don't know what you're—"

"Just leave me alone."

I want to sink into the floor and shrivel up. We'd argued earlier because I'd promised to take her to an art museum, but my work schedule had changed at the last minute, forcing me to cover an afternoon shift at the bookstore. I'd apologized, but she'd forgotten that conversation, and now we were back to the beginning again, rewinding the tape and playing the same track over and over.

I go into my room and shut the door, climb into my bed, and cover my head with a pillow. Ten minutes pass by, and I can't sleep yet. Then I hear shuffling noises, see bare feet on the floor by my bed.

Uncovering my head, I look up at her. "Hi, Mom."

"I've done everything for you, Nina." Her voice is quiet, even. "I worked so hard to take care of you after your father died. I worked full time, I helped you with your homework, I fed you, I put a roof over your head. And then I ask you to do one simple thing, and at the last minute you back out on me."

"I'm sorry, Mom."

The gripping pain takes hold of my chest, squeezing. It radiates outward, cutting through my arms and legs, making every cell in my body squirm. It's as if I'm trying to escape myself, and I wonder if now would be a good time to drift out of my skin. I remember my therapist, the only one I ever had, whom I haven't seen in three years, and I wish I could still see him, get his thoughts on this. But to do that I'd have to—

"You are nothing but a manipulative bitch." The words emerge in a snarl. She leans over me, her hands on her hips.

Then she stomps out of the room, and I'm alone. I listen to sirens blaring somewhere in the distance and watch the play of headlights against the ceiling of my room. I drift into a heavy slumber, my face wet with tears, my mind plagued with nightmares.

I wake in the morning groggy and delirious, the pain in my chest ever present. It doesn't go away until after my morning coffee and bagel, followed by a kiss on the cheek from my cheerful mother, who cannot remember last night.

***

I dig my toes into the sand, and the heat radiates up through the soles of my feet. I think of my mother and how much I love her when she's sober. I'm not sure who she is when she's drinking—someone else, someone I don't know.

Now I'm waiting for someone I don't know *very well*—Wes, who called to see what I was up to. He lives in Cocoa Beach, two hours away, and he's in the area visiting friends.

It's Saturday, and I'm scheduled off from the bookstore, so there's nowhere else I'd rather be than here, watching a sailboat in the distance, the puffy clouds in the sky, the people walking their dogs out past Juno Pier. I can't help but be elated, content, as if I'm floating with those clouds, weightless and free.

My fingers are hooked around my flip-flops, and I'm wearing a white tank top and black running shorts. Just as I'm thinking about taking a jog down to the water, I hear someone move behind me.

"Hey, Nina." Wes steps up beside me, wearing a t-shirt and shorts. It looks as if he's left his shoes in his car. Dark sunglasses cover his eyes, and the breeze tosses an errant curl over his left eye. The dimples form in his cheeks when he smiles, and for a split second I wonder what it would be like to kiss that part of his face, where the dimple meets the scruffy beginnings of a beard he'll probably shave off by tomorrow morning.

I shake the thought out of my mind as quickly as it pops into existence, almost as if I'm worried he'll read it. Shy, I cross my left arm over my body and scratch at my elbow, even though it doesn't itch.

"Want to go for a walk?" I ask, desperate to do something that will take my mind away from him. I'm afraid if we exchange too many glances, he'll know what I'm thinking, or something will happen I'm not prepared for.

He nods, and we walk along the beach, discovering treasure troves of shells that washed up during yesterday's rain. I reach down and scoop up a spiral-shaped shell, small, no more than an inch and a half long, and marvel at its beauty.

"I hardly ever find ones like this," I say, showing it to him. "Isn't it pretty?"

"Yeah, there are so many today, you can hardly see the sand in this spot."

He's right. They rub together under our feet, and when the surf washes up, it tosses all the shells together, making it sound as if Poseidon is playing a tune we might dance to.

We stand for a moment and stare at the water. "I like to watch the waves wash up," I muse. "If I stare at the water long enough, I'm mesmerized. I feel like I'm drifting out of my body, like I did at the race."

"You told me about that. You should be careful."

"I know. That's what my therapist said. I used to do that stuff all the time, drifting out of my mind and telling myself stories when I was a kid, but I didn't know it had a name." I look at Wes, shaking my head. "I don't see what the big deal is, but my therapist said to me, 'Nina, dissociation is a defense mechanism, you need to think about why you do this.'"

"And did you?"

"To a point. But I think I know why I do it."

"Why?" Wes reaches down and picks up another spiral shell before slipping it into my hand. When our fingers touch, I shiver.

"I mentioned I grew up in dysfunction, more than most people. I know nothing's perfect, but I had to take care of my mother. She took care of me too, but sometimes I felt like our roles were reversed.

"She's such a wonderful woman, Wes. But when she drinks she becomes...someone else. She's a writer like me, but she doesn't think much of anything she does. She's really good, but she doesn't believe it." I glance at him, shrugging. "And I didn't have any friends growing up, so I learned to be my own friend, make up stories, create characters. Maybe she did the same thing, maybe we're the same that way. I guess you could say writing in itself is a defense mechanism for me."

"I can see that. In some ways, I'm sure it is for me too. Did you tell your therapist that?"

"I don't see him anymore. He...he had to quit the practice."

"Oh," Wes says, and I'm grateful he doesn't ask me about it. I don't want to go into the whole story. Then I'd have to tell him why I went to a therapist in the first place.

"I haven't spent this much time here in a while," I say. We walk slowly along, finding a stretch of beach where smooth rock formations, like sandstone, create circular pools of water. We watch as the sea spray jumps up through the rocks, covering our feet when we stand in between them.

"When was the last time you were here? Before the race, I mean," Wes asks, scooping up a few more shells, examining them, dropping whichever ones he doesn't want.

"Last week, but not for very long. I got home from work, and Mom wanted to go to the beach." I sigh, reach up, and rub my hand across my neck, another action reserved for moments like this when I don't know what to do with my hands, a nervous habit like scratching at my elbow or playing with my earrings. "She wouldn't leave me alone. I was trying to write, and she kept barging in my room."

"Lock the door?" He snickers.

"It wouldn't do any good. She just knocks and yells at me until I open it. If I don't, the yelling turns into screaming." At his perplexed expression, I explain, "She starts drinking around three. She's retired now, so she's home during the day. Which is fine, I love her when she's sober. She's the best mom a girl could ask for. Until the bottle comes out." I sit down on one of the massive rocks, and Wes sits across from me. "She yelled at me and badgered me until I agreed to bring her here, but I didn't realize until we got here that she was drunk. We started walking toward the beach, and she stumbled and almost fell in the bushes."

"What'd you do?"

"What I always do. I grabbed her arm to steady her, and she swatted me away and said she didn't need my help. I told her she was drunk, and she got even more pissed at me. I was so scared someone would see us, so embarrassed."

"I don't blame you. I can't imagine what that's like. But you have to remember it's not your fault, and no one is going to blame you for her behavior. Forget what other people think. Fuck 'em. They don't matter."

I see her in my memory, just before we leave the beach, walking down to the water to *say goodbye to mother ocean*, to feel the salty froth against her feet. She bows, her dress blowing around her, looking like a Pagan priestess reciting an ancient rite, her hands clasped together in prayer, *thank you, mother ocean, thank you for your blessings*, and she stumbles as a wave reaches up. I dart forward as if to save her from herself, my fingers wrapping around her thin, bony arm, and with her other hand she waves me away, annoyance flashing in her dark eyes. *Leave me alone,* they demand. I could do as she asks, but it would mean leaving her here, on the beach, in the light of the setting sun, to sleep amongst the sea grapes and the spotted skunks.

"Nina?"

I feel warmth against my hand and realize he's touching me, rousing me from my reverie. My gaze fixes on the water as it washes against the rocks; I'd lost myself in thought, drifted away from him. Not quite dissociation, but something close.

"I'm sorry. I don't mean to dump all this on you. We only just met and—"

"I don't mind. I'm a writer. I like listening to other people's stories," he reminds me, and his words sound so much like words I've told other people, over and over, for many years, that it's almost like I'm listening to myself. I tell him as much, and he laughs. "We have a lot in common, Nina."

"I know." I purse my lips together, but I'm unable to stop the small smile from lifting my cheeks up. "What are you going to do, put me into a story?" I narrow my eyes at him.

"Maybe, you'd better watch out," he jokes. We laugh together and climb up from our seats to continue our walk.

"I just don't know how much longer I can live with her. I'm not sure how much longer I can put up with it."

"I know," he says, slipping his hand in mine.

Chapter 5

I haven't worn the cross in years, but tonight is special. It's Christmas Eve, and I'm going to see my friend Jenny perform with her choir. We remained close friends over the years, and I've even told her about my home life. I was afraid she'd think less of me, but she didn't.

My cell phone vibrates as a text message comes through:

You're coming, right?

Of course. I wouldn't miss it for the world.

I haven't been in a church since I was a teenager. I'd gone once with my grandparents, and my mother had complained about it, insisting they were attempting to brainwash me, when all I wanted was to spend time with them.

On my way out the door, I say goodbye to my mother. "I'll be home late," I warn.

"What's with the cross?" Mom flicks the pendant, and I feel it slip softly against my skin.

"Don't you remember? Jenny got it for me when we were in high school."

"Hmm. Where are you going?"

"To church."

"What for?"

"To see Jenny sing. Anyway, what's wrong with that?"

Mom says nothing. She just goes back to the Fern Michaels novel she was reading, and I walk out the door.

***

I never met my grandfather, but I've heard a lot about him.

He touched Mom in places no father should touch his daughter, creeping into her room at night and playing games with her mind and body. She's never gotten past it.

On Sundays he took his family to church, and they all sat together in the pew. Everyone liked him. He was an upstanding member of the congregation, always involved in his community. No one would have guessed what he did in the dark when no one was looking.

Mom thought it was normal, so she didn't say a word until after he died, finally speaking up after years of torment. By then she'd taken to the bottle, the only source of comfort that didn't abandon her as her father had. And every time she saw a church, the child inside her wept. If she heard the music of an organ on the television or radio, she would cover her ears and shriek, "I hate it, I hate it! Turn it off!"

So, I understood. I knew why she did what she did. And my heart broke for her.

My heart still breaks for her.

Although the rape haunts me, I try to work through it. Every day, I'm trying, working to transform into a new version of myself—a woman who is no longer afraid of being touched, of intimacy.

I could easily slip into the bottle as well. But I refuse to.

In the church, I sit by myself and look up at the stage, where they've set up a beautiful arrangement of poinsettias and lights. The piano is decked out in greenery, and the tree in the corner is bright and cheerful. As people begin to file in, my chest tightens, and I knit my fingers together in my lap. Someone asks if the seat beside me is taken, and I say no. The chunky woman plops into the chair next to me, and I shift a little to give her room. She drops a heavy purse before her and leans back. Being so close to strangers makes me want to leave. I put one leg over the other and cross my arms loosely over my chest, already checking my watch to see when the show will end.

The music begins, and I see Jenny in the first row, her long black hair hanging straight behind her, her graceful figure clad in red to match the rest of the choir. I smile at her and wave, and she winks in reply. They sing *Jingle Bells* and *Little Drummer Boy* and some other songs I'm not familiar with.

I feel awkward, as if everyone in the room is turning and looking at me, mouthing the words, "She doesn't go to church. She doesn't belong here." But when I glance around, no one's looking at me. They're all looking up front, listening to the lilting melodies that fill the room with holiday cheer. I know I'm uncomfortable because I've been trained to be, and I think of my mother and how she clenches the steering wheel tighter when we drive by a church, how her thin lips tighten as she looks away.

The pastor talks about Jesus, the son of God, and mentions stories from the Bible I've never heard of. I feel as if they know I'm ignorant somehow. I look around at the sea of faces, and so many people are nodding their understanding. As my stomach ties itself in knots, I wonder why these words bother me.

Then I think back.

Mom drunk on Christmas. Sobbing, talking about her father. The abuse. The beatings. Rage spewing forth as she slams her fist on the drab maroon carpeting.

Never forgive anyone. It's a Christian concept. The Bible is full of lies. Church is just where people are manipulated into sheep.

A little boy hands out candles, and a person at the end of each aisle helps us light them. Soon every person in the room is holding a bright little flame, and I'm watching mine leap, slowly melting the top of the candle until there's a glimmering drop of wax threatening to fall.

The pastor leads us in a meditation.

Bring the light of Jesus into you, radiate that light…carry the light wherever you go, and share it with the world.

I breathe in, and something changes. I let the light in.

Mom. You did this. You gave me all these negative thoughts. I don't want them anymore.

I'm not sure I believe in Jesus, and I'm not sure I'm religious, but I let the light flare up inside me. If there is a Jesus, I let Him into my heart.

After the service, I hug Jenny, congratulate her, and wait in line to leave the building. Beside me is the woman I sat next to, beaming with joy.

"Do you come to this church regularly?" she asks me, placing a gentle hand on my shoulder.

"No," I say, shaking my head.

"Oh, you go to another church?"

I shake my head again.

"Oh," the woman says, moving her hand away, turning her head.

I walk out of the bright, colorful building and into the darkness, where I climb into my car and drive home, relieved to be heading back to something I'm familiar with—something comfortable.

At least I won't be there much longer.

***

We recline on the Mexican blanket I brought from my car, and I stretch my legs out to dig my feet into the sand. I think of when I was little, sprawled out on the beach, and my mother sat in a chair watching me, her travel mug filled with wine instead of coffee. At the time, I'd wondered if it was possible to dig my way to China, so I tried, but I didn't get very far. Now I remember hearing someone say even if it were possible to dig clear through the world, no matter where you dug from, you'd never end up in China.

"Looks like there's a storm out there," I say, nodding toward the horizon. Dark clouds gather over the ocean, turning the water a surreal pale blue, and I can see the rain far off in the distance, manifesting itself in streaks of color that slant toward the sea.

Wes turns his head to glance behind us. "It's sunny back there. I doubt the storm will reach us."

"Don't be so sure. You never know."

"That's true."

We both lay back, enjoying each other's company, not saying much. The heat rests over us like a comforting blanket. I wouldn't trade this moment for anything.

Out of the corner of my eye, I catch a movement. There's a young girl fishing by the surf, her ocean pole held expertly in her small hands.

"I have to tell you something." I turn my head to Wes. He looks at me, then we shift on our sides to face each other. My head presses against the blanket, my right arm under my body, my legs bent and resting comfortably. I could fall asleep like this.

Our gazes meet. Something about his dark brown eyes is too much for me, as if he's looking into me, into my mind, reading my thoughts.

"What's up?" he asks, his expression playful. He's rolling a little orange-and-white shell around in his hands.

"I'm moving to North Carolina next month."

His lips part slightly, and for a moment he looks shocked, then disappointed. "But I just met you. Another writer here in Florida. Why are you leaving?"

"I found a cheap apartment in a good part of town, and a friend of mine manages a bookstore there. She promised me a job."

"You don't have to go. You can find a place here. I have a cousin who's a real estate agent."

"I already sent in my deposit."

Can I go back on that? I wonder. Can I contact the building manager, get my money back? Or will they have to keep some of it for the trouble I caused them? No—I already committed. I can't pull out. Can I?

I wonder why I would. What would be my reason for staying here? Certainly not for a man I just met, a guy I've known a little over a week. There's an ache somewhere in my heart, and I ponder why. Am I falling for him? And how can I possibly trust such a childish yearning?

I realize he's watching me intently. When I look at him for longer than a second, I begin to panic. Something inside me wants to get up and leave, yet I can't put my finger on why.

"This sucks." He drops the shell on the blanket, then rolls onto his back.

I lay on my back, too, staring up at the sky.

There's something else we both want to say, but neither of us has the words. Many moments pass in silence, until we hear a yell, then a splashing. I sit up.

"Look," I say, pointing. He rises, crossing his legs, and we watch.

The girl's fishing pole is bending nearly in half, and she calls out to someone as she leans back, pulling, digging her bare feet into the sand. A man rushes up and grabs hold of her, helping steady the pole. Together they pull.

"Reel it in!" he shouts.

People gather, watching.

A shape is dragged through the water, splashing and fighting.

"Oh my God," I mutter, and beside me Wes is gaping.

The shark is as big as she is, maybe bigger, gray and white; it lays on the sand, unmoving. People gather and snap photos while we sit and stare, amazed. The man approaches the shark and releases the line, though I can't tell if he's brave enough to get the hook out of the creature's mouth. Maybe it's in shock, frozen in fear.

I know what that's like.

Soon they're rolling it back out to sea, pushing it away, and it returns to life, flipping its tail, heading home.

I wonder what it's like to be released from pain, allowed to swim free.

One day, that will be me.

The beach is quiet again; there aren't many people around. Maybe because they think it's going to start pouring. I don't mind. I'd rather get caught in the rain than walk away.

"I have something else to tell you," I say.

"Oh no. You're joining the circus?"

"No, don't be silly." I reach forward and draw shapes in the sand, digging my feet deeper into the warm, soft granules.

"Then what?"

I glance over at him, smiling wryly. "Promise you won't think I'm crazy?"

"Cross my heart."

"Okay, here goes." I look away when I tell him, because I'm afraid of what he'll say. "A year ago I had a dream, and you were in it. I've been thinking a lot about it, and I know it was you." I look at him, shyly, and catch his gaze. "It's your eyes. They're the same. But you looked different in the dream. You were a different person. At first I thought it was someone in this life, but now I see it was a past life. Do you believe in past lives?"

Wes shrugs. "I'm not sure what I believe in. I never really thought about past lives. I just believe in the universe providing what we need, and I think everyone's energy is connected somehow."

"Carl Jung. The collective unconscious."

"Yes, exactly."

Suddenly I like him even more, because he knows who Carl Jung is. Smirking, I continue, "Well, in this dream, you and I were together in a room. It was like a hotel. You said my name, but it was a different name, I know that now."

"A hotel room? What were we doing?"

I punch him playfully on the shoulder. "Stop it."

"You're blushing. We must have been doing something."

"How do you know I'm not just getting sunburn?" I stick out my tongue at him, and he laughs.

"Tell me the rest."

"There wasn't much more. You had to go to war, and you left. It was the last time I saw you. At the end of the dream, I saw you standing on a dirt road, forest on one side. Someone shot you in the chest, and you fell, calling out my name. Then your body disappeared, and all these flags appeared along the road. They were American flags, but they looked different, and each little flag represented a fallen soldier."

"Wow. You know, I almost joined the Army once."

"What made you change your mind?"

"My girlfriend at the time talked me out of it."

"Oh."

"I sometimes wish I'd gone, but I've had such a good life just being here, and traveling, and living in Cocoa Beach, I'm glad now I didn't."

"I have prophetic dreams sometimes. I hope you don't think I'm crazy."

"Not at all." He turns to face me. "I have dreams like that too."

"Really?"

"Remember after the race, when I brushed your hair out of your eyes?"

"Yes." I glance down at the ground, feeling my face flush. "What about it?"

39

"I realized why you looked so familiar to me. I had a dream about you before I met you." When I say nothing, he continues, "In the dream, a man's voice said I was going to meet a writer. He asked if I would like to see her before I met her, and I said yes. All of a sudden I was standing on a beach like this one, with no one else around, and I saw you by the surf. Your hair was down and you were wearing a blue sundress. When I walked up to you…"

"Yes?"

"I kissed you."

Blushing, I dig my feet deeper in the sand, as if to distract myself from his words. "Oh," I mumble.

"Can I kiss you now, Nina?"

"Wes…"

"Don't be nervous." He slips his hand around mine, gently stroking my knuckles. "It's obvious there's an attraction between us. It's natural." He scoots closer to me on the blanket.

"I…I don't know." I think of North Carolina. Why start something that will have to end?

Soon he's so close his bare arm is brushing against mine and I feel his muscles tense. When he leans in, his breath on my skin, he feathers a gentle kiss on my cheek. My body feels as if it's on fire, and I clench my legs together, goose bumps rising on my skin, nipples hardening. My body is reacting while my mind screams *stop*.

Go away, go away…don't…stay…

The sounds around me dissipate. Children yelling, playing down by the water. Joggers chatting as they run by. A horn honking out on the road behind us.

When I Dream of You

I turn my head and my lips meet his, gentle at first, making it seem like an eternity in which we're just sitting there, our lips pressed together, our bodies so close I can hardly stand it. Then I feel his tongue against mine, and I reach out, tasting him. His kisses are hard and tender at the same time, and I've never had anything sweeter than this. His hair gently brushes my forehead as I tilt to the side, allowing him in, deeper, as his arm slips around my waist.

We kiss like this for a while, and then he draws himself away, and I'm left sitting there with my eyes half shut, my heart hammering, a chill making me shiver even though it's eighty-five degrees in the sun. When I open my eyes, I'm looking at him, and he's smiling with a glimmer of excitement, pleased with himself, as if he's been thinking about trying this since the first moment we met.

"Are you sure you want to go to North Carolina?"

I shake my head. "No. No, I'm not sure."

I lie back on the blanket, and he holds my hand, linking his fingers with mine.

Chapter 6

Twelve years ago

The light is dim, yellowish, as I sit on my mother's bed telling her why she shouldn't kill herself.

"I love you, Mom. I need you. Please don't die."

My mother sobs, punching her fists into the pillow. "I just want to die, I just want to kill myself."

"Please stop talking like that."

I sit on the edge of her bed rubbing her back. She quiets down for a while, but then starts sobbing again.

"Why did he do that to me?"

"Who, Mom?"

"My father. The way he touched me...why?"

"I don't know."

She is up before I realize what she's doing. Sinking to the floor, she throws herself against the wall, slamming her head into the drywall. I jump into action, rushing toward her. She's stronger than she looks. I can't pull her away, and she tries to fight back, pushing me—

"Get away from me, let me go!"

"Mom, stop, you can't...you'll hurt yourself!"

Her face stained with tears, she slams her head forward again, harder this time, and without much recourse I force myself in front of her, getting between her and the wall.

Let her hit me, I can handle it.

She throws herself against me, but then falls back on her heels and digs her fingers into her scalp, her hair sticking out in all directions. I know she'll wear herself out eventually, she always does. I put my arms around her and hold her for a long time, letting her sob on my shoulder. Soon she quiets down, and I help her into bed, tucking her in as though she were a small child. She curls up, her head on the pillow, her eyes shut.

"Nina."

"Yes, Mom."

"I love you."

"I love you, too."

"You know." Mom nuzzles the pillow, fluffing it beneath her with one hand before tugging the blanket up to her chin. "I would have killed myself long ago if it weren't for you."

"I know, Mom." A sharp pain passes through me. It hurts me every time I hear it, but I can't explain why.

Late at night, once she's tucked away in her bed, sleeping soundly, I creep out of the apartment and walk downstairs. Outside, a full moon reflects on the water of the intracoastal. I step through the dewy grass in my bare feet, heedless of the fire ants and lizards skittering ahead of me.

Sitting by the water, I enjoy a brief moment of privacy, in which no one knows I am there, in the dark, picturing a better life. A life in which my mother is sober, I am happy, and my father is alive. It's not often I allow the tears to come. But tonight, with only the moon to keep me company, I weep, wiping my eyes with the back of my hand.

I don't know what it's like to enjoy coming home, to look forward to being in my bedroom. I have no privacy there, where I lock the door and she picks it with a coat hanger, no matter how many times I ask her not to. When I want to be alone, really alone, I take a shower. I stand there in the stall, letting the water hit me, just leaning against the wall and thinking. Sometimes I cry there. The shower doesn't always afford the privacy I need; she picks that lock, too. But most of the time I can hide there.

Now I cry by the water, giving my tears to the brackish liquid below me. After a while, I go upstairs, my face red, my skin puffy. The apartment is dark. A gentle breeze blows through the open windows. I step into my mother's room, and see her curled up on the bed.

Walking closer, I look at her face under the glow of the streetlights that permeate the dirty windows. She's not moving. Her chest is motionless beneath her nightshirt. I place my hand under her nose to make sure she's alive, as I have many times in the past.

When I Dream of You

She stirs in her sleep, breathes deep. I relax. *She's okay.*

Wringing my hands, I step back, and go quietly to my bedroom to climb under the blankets where I toss and turn, frightened she'll die in her sleep.

Chapter 7

One week ago, Jupiter, Florida

"Are you going to just sit there and stare at your coffee, or are you going to drink it?"

I glance up at Jenny, who is eyeing me with an expression of intense consternation. She's always been very perceptive.

"You'd be a great detective, you know that? The question is, would you be the good cop or the bad cop?"

"Nina, I have never seen you just sit there and stare at your coffee. You *love* coffee. You chug the stuff. And here you are, staring at it. Why?"

We're sitting in a café in Juno Beach, tucked into a corner at a little table, scooting to the side whenever a patron squeezes between us and the counter while on the way to the bathroom. We are in close enough proximity that we can hear toilet lids slamming down, and I consider using that as an excuse for not indulging in my caffeinated beverage, but I know Jenny will never fall for it. She knows nothing could stop me from enjoying my java.

I finally sip it and lean back in my chair, holding the cup in both hands. "I don't know. I'm worried about this move."

"I thought you were excited about North Carolina. You've always wanted to live there."

"Yeah, I was excited. I still want to go. But what if I'm making the wrong decision?"

"No decision is wrong, Nina. You can't be everywhere at once. What are you going to miss out on here that you can't have in North Carolina?" She frowns, coming to the conclusion on her own. "It's a guy, isn't it?"

I feel my cheeks burn. "Yes."

"Who?"

"His name is Wes. I met him at the race last week. We hit it off immediately. Only he lives in Cocoa Beach, and here I am moving—"

Jenny reaches across the table and takes my hand, gently squeezing my fingers. "Honey, you've got to follow your heart. But be careful. You haven't known this guy very long."

"I know, but I dreamt about him a year ago."

"Really?"

Jenny knows my dreams, and she believes me. I nod.

"Well, tell me. What happened?" Jenny asks, leaning forward, her eyes wide.

I describe the dream in detail, telling her what I'd left out when I told Wes. I couldn't tell him we'd made love, and that it was so passionate the

47

dream lasted all night, and in the morning I awoke wet between my legs until I realized he was dead, and then I sobbed, grief-stricken, my heart broken, my chest aflame with aches and pains that didn't go away for hours. He wouldn't have understood. Would he?

"Wow." Jenny releases my hand and is leaning on her palms, her elbows against the table. "That's amazing."

"That's not all. He dreamt about me too."

"He did?"

"Yeah. He saw me in a dream right before we met. In his dream, we kissed."

Jenny smirks. "You think he left out some dirty stuff, like you did?"

"Oh, come on. It's not dirty. I just...I can't talk to him about that stuff."

She flashes her white teeth, full lips shiny and pink. "Oh, you will."

"No, I won't. I'm moving, remember?"

"How do you know? Maybe it's fate." Jenny sips her coffee, and I say nothing.

We exchange a glance, and I know what she's thinking.

Make up your mind, Nina. Make up your mind.

***

We're meeting on the beach again. But this time I'm surprising him with a picnic lunch, and I'm frantic, worried he won't like the sandwiches I made, or the drinks I brought, or the snacks I grabbed at the last minute.

I consider the fact I never asked him if he was allergic to anything, and I don't know his favorite foods. A little voice in my head screams, *you don't even know him very well*, but I try to ignore it as I clutch the picnic basket tightly, and walk across the parking lot at Jupiter Beach Park, my flip flops slapping the bottoms of my feet.

I bite my bottom lip as I pass by a group of young guys who are laughing and smoking cigarettes. I avert my eyes. Ever since the rape, men make me uncomfortable, and I'd almost always rather stay home than come across them in a bar or a social setting. There's a terrified part of me that says they'll just use me and toss me away like a piece of trash. And I can't have that. I can't let it happen to me again.

So I avoid them.

Which is why it's strange I've met Wes.

I walk along the path that leads to the beach, and I see him waiting there, standing in the sand, leaning against the railing. He hasn't spotted me yet, so I slow down. He's not wearing a shirt, just his swimming shorts and sandals, and he's looking out over the beach, his eyes covered by his sunglasses.

He has a runner's body, lean and muscular, and the breeze is tossing back his dark curls. I bite my lip again, and force myself to continue. He turns and catches my eye, and I smile, still shy, still nervous.

"Hey, what do you have there?" he asks, walking toward me. When he's close enough, he touches my elbows, the basket between us, and leans forward to place a gentle kiss on my cheek. I shiver in response. "You can't be cold in this weather?" he jokes.

"No." I glance down toward the ground. "Just nervous."

"You don't have to be nervous around me. Haven't I told you that before?"

"I'm not sure."

We walk out on the beach, and I hand him the blanket. He spreads it out on the sand, and I place the basket on top.

"Are you hungry?" I ask.

"Did you make me lunch?" He sits down, and I follow suit.

"Yes, is that okay?"

"Is it okay—it's fantastic. I can't believe you did that for me."

I blush. "It's just sandwiches, that's all."

"Even so. It was very sweet of you."

We sit and eat, and I keep thinking how uncomfortable I am eating in front of him, as if I'm worried a glob of mustard is going to fall on my shirt, or I'm going to make a mess, or maybe I sound funny when I chew, or—

My mind runs in circles, and I can't keep up. I think of Jenny and what we talked about in the café, and then I think about North Carolina. I'm moving next month. Wes would go back to Cocoa Beach in a couple of days, and whatever was between us would be gone, fallen to dust that would mix with the sand, to be blown away on the next strong wind.

Halfway through my sandwich, I sit cross-legged and stare at the ocean. "I can't believe I'm moving next month." I turn and look at him, trying to seem casual when I ask, "Will I see you again?"

"I don't know if I'll be back in the area before then, Nina."

"Oh."

I watch some kids throw a ball back and forth, and for a moment I wonder if they'll accidentally hit it in the wrong direction and it'll come sailing toward me and smack me in the head. Just as I'm thinking this, Wes clears his throat.

"You know, you don't have to move to North Carolina. You could come with me. I'm going to Sweden this summer to research a book I'm writing."

"Are you asking me to go with you?"

"Yeah." He smirks. "Run away with me, Nina."

I gulp. "Run away? I don't know. I've never done anything like that before."

"Which is precisely why you should."

I turn and look out at the water again, then take another bite of my sandwich. When I finish chewing, I say, "Let me think about it," and that's the last he mentions it for the rest of the day.

Chapter 8

Deep in slumber, I see his face. I dream we're driving somewhere, but I don't know where we are, and we're speeding around turns, winding around other vehicles, and he's driving. I reach out as if to slow us down, but I have no control.

"Wes, please be careful, this is too fast!" I shout, but he doesn't seem to hear me; he just presses on the pedal and flies around a turn, and I see palm trees around us, and tall buildings. Are we in Miami, Daytona? I can't tell. "Wes, slow down, slow down!"

We narrowly miss an eighteen-wheeler, and I shriek, sweating, my heart palpitating.

He turns and looks at me, and somehow we stay on the road, we're moving, but he's not paying attention to where we're going, and he says, "It doesn't matter, Nina. It's fate. You can't stop it."

"No, no!" There's a cement wall ahead. "Wes, watch out!"

"Don't worry. With impact comes change."

We slam into the wall and—

I jolt in my bed, my whole body shuddering, my eyes fluttering open. I hear a noise and for a moment I wonder what it is. Then I realize it's my phone vibrating on the end table, and I roll over, reaching out, fumbling to pick it up.

"H-hello?"

"Nina, I hope I didn't wake you."

"Who...w-who's this?"

The woman on the other line laughs. "Don't you recognize my voice? It's your boss, silly. We've only been working together for six years."

"Oh. Hi, Lynn." I stretch out on my back, still under the covers. "I was sleeping."

"I'm so sorry I woke you."

"It's okay, not a big deal. What's up?"

"I had to call early. Yesterday was slow, and I don't anticipate today will very busy, so I thought I'd let you know you don't have to come in today."

"Oh. Wow, thanks."

"I'll let you go back to sleep."

"No, I can't now," I say, chuckling.

"Aww," Lynn says, sounding apologetic. A beautiful blonde with twinkling blue eyes, Lynn is older than me by ten years, and one of the sweetest people I've ever known. Even when I make mistakes at work, she admonishes me with such kindness it's difficult to be disappointed with her. She pauses for a moment, then adds, "Well, I'll see you in a couple of days."

"Okay, sounds good." I remember I have time off, and it's New Year's Eve.

53

After hanging up the phone and sliding it onto the end table, I lie back and think about my resolutions. I have none. What do I want for the new year? I'm not sure. The clock on the wall tells me it's six in the morning. I begin thinking about what I will do that day, and I know I have to drive to the grocery store.

Drive.

My dream flashes back to me. I cringe at the thought of slamming into that cement, and I am glad I woke up. I've always had nightmares. Being in a situation I have no control over is terrifying to me, just as frightening as the rape, which is always in the back of my mind no matter what I do to try to expel it.

Wes's words in the dream, so clear—*It doesn't matter, Nina. It's fate. You can't stop it.*

With impact comes change.

I sink into my pillow, staring up at the white ceiling. The blankets are warm, but I feel cold inside.

"I don't believe in fate, Wes," I whisper softly. "I *can* stop it if I want."

But I wasn't so sure that was true.

My eyes flutter shut, and before I know it I'm asleep again. I don't wake up until eight o' clock, my neck aching, my head pounding, groggy and in need of coffee.

In the kitchen, I watch it brewing and listen as it bubbles and hisses, the condo filling with a heady aroma. My mother walks in wearing a pair of jean shorts and a t-shirt, a quartz crystal hanging around her neck, her short hair neatly combed.

"Good morning, sweetheart." She kisses me on the cheek, and her breath smells minty and sweet. She squeezes my shoulders gently and peers at my face before brushing my hair away from my neck and tucking strands behind my ear. "Are you all right?"

"Mmm-hmm. Why, Mom?" I put my arm around her, leaning on her shoulder. I wish she were like this all the time.

"You were talking in your sleep and crying out. I went in your room early this morning. You were on your side, so I rubbed your back. It seemed to calm you down. I just hope you're not going through anything difficult right now. You work so much, we don't get time to talk like we used to."

"I know, Mommy," I whisper, feeling like a child again. I want to cry as I think of the two personalities my mother harbors, the angry alcoholic and the loving, beautiful woman I see in the morning, who makes pancakes for me on my birthday and drinks tea while reading Nora Roberts novels. Where does that woman go in the evening? Where does she hide?

"What are you up to today, dear?"

"I don't know, Mom. Probably just hang out, maybe go to the beach."

"You've been going to the beach a lot lately, more than usual."

I think of Wes, and smile. "Yeah, I know. I love the beach."

I pour a cup of coffee, and then go back to my room. Sinking onto my mattress, I pick up my cell phone. I key in a text message and press *send*.

Hey, Wes. Hope you're having a nice morning. I know it's kinda early, but I was wondering what you're up to today.

I sip my coffee, staring out the window, and my phone buzzes a moment later.

Headed back to Cocoa Beach last night. Had an emergency, a friend's car broke down and she doesn't have anybody else in the area to help her.

I slump my shoulders, saddened. But why am I letting it bother me? I have to remind myself I'm moving soon, and I can't get too involved with him, can't let myself fall for him. Then I remember my dream.

Fate.

"No," I tell myself. "There's no such thing."

There couldn't be. I wouldn't allow it.

***

Control. It frightens me. And if fate exists, that means I have no control.

Trapped under his heaving body while he raped me, laughing when I resisted, I'd lost control. Any similar situation caused a flashback, and I was back there instantly, crushed against that broken spring, begging him to stop.

I remember what my therapist called it—*post traumatic stress disorder*. In his office, sitting in a cozy armchair, I learned why I was so afraid of

56

men. I wish I could talk to him now, but he's gone. He did a bad thing, but he was the only one who listened to me. I wonder why he made those mistakes, landed himself in jail, a man who'd helped countless young girls work through their troubled pasts.

I will never know the answer to this.

New Year's Eve.

Fireworks burst in the sky over the intracoastal. We don't have to leave the house for the show. In the darkened condo, the walls light up with red, yellow, blue, pink, white, and purple. My mother stands on the balcony wearing a sundress, a cup in her hand. I know it's not water she's drinking.

I'm in the kitchen when I hear the loud noises, the motor of the boat rumbling, the music blaring as the neighbors return from their excursion. It's around nine or ten, so maybe they're picking something up from the condo downstairs—more alcohol perhaps. I don't have anyone to party with, or maybe I'd be somewhere drinking a beer or a shot.

I'm making a sandwich when I hear my mother shrieking, and I turn to see her shadowy form briefly illuminated by lights from the outdoors, fireworks blasting beyond her like exploding stars.

"Shut up! Shut the fuck up!" She's screeching down to the boaters as she leans over the railing.

I cringe. She's done this before. She hates them, and how they have no respect for their neighbors, coming home at all hours and playing the radio so loud it shakes the windows. But what she does is just as bad, and I feel more humiliated than ever, my heart pounding as I grow small, recalling similar incidents from my childhood when I tried to protect her from herself.

I drop what I'm doing and walk across the living room.

"Don't you hear me? Shut the fuck up!"

On the balcony, I grab her arm, gentle, trying to coax her back in. "Mom—"

"Get the hell off me!"

"Mom, stop screaming at them, they can't even hear you!" I yell over the music.

"These assholes won't shut up!" She shouts in my face, her breath heavy with liquor.

"You're only making it worse, Mom." I put my arm around her to get her back inside, but she shoves me away.

"Stop it! What do I look like to you, a child?" She nearly trips on the chair beside her, and I reach out to steady her, which only makes her angrier. She shoves me, I stumble against the glass door, and it shudders with my weight.

My whole body heats up, and tears well in my eyes, but I refuse to let them fall. For many years we've played this game, as I try to keep her from humiliating herself—to keep her from embarrassing me—but nothing does any good, and nothing ever changes. I clench my hands into fists, remembering how I broke through my flesh at the race, blood trickling along my palms. I want to bleed now, to let go of this pain, and it's moments like this I envision myself sinking into the water below, finding the peacefulness of death, residing forever at the silted bottom where all is quiet.

This isn't like me. I'm a good, happy person—or I used to be. But living with her, I can't reach my full potential, and I know it.

North Carolina. I have to get out of here.

She's yelling again, but this time the music is off, and they're unloading the boat.

"Don't you have any goddamn respect for anyone? What's wrong with you?" She brandishes a finger at them, 'pointing over the railing, and they stare up at her—three men and two women—with bemused expressions on their faces. Every time they try to defend themselves, she shouts over them. "Just shut the fuck up, get your shit out of here, I don't want to hear this..."

"Mom! Stop!"

"Oh my God, I can't take this anymore!" She throws her fists in the air, then drags her broken fingernails through her hair and stomps off the balcony, through the living room, and to her bedroom.

I lean over the railing and see three people looking up at me, raising their shoulders, waiting for an explanation. The other two have wandered off. I make a motion like someone drinking from a bottle, then twirl my index finger around my ear.

"I'm sorry," I call down to them.

The blonde in Daisy Dukes waves a small hand. "It's okay. I know what it's like. My dad's that way."

The guys say goodnight, and one of them even says good luck. When they've gone inside, I trudge off the balcony and shut the sliding glass doors. I wonder what they think of me, then I remind myself of Wes's advice.

But you have to remember it's not your fault, and no one is going to blame you for her behavior.

I walk through the darkened hallway. It's getting late, nearly ten-thirty now.

I wonder if it's fate that my mother drinks, or if it's fate that she'll never quit. Will she die of alcohol poisoning? Will I have to bury my mother knowing she was never able to heal, never able to let go of her childhood abuse? The thought makes me shudder. I know how the rape affected me, but I try to work through it, and I never find solace at the bottom of a bottle, just a sour stomach and a hangover.

Not worth it. Even if it makes the pain go away just a little bit. Nothing is worth this.

As I near my bedroom door, she opens her own door and leans against the frame, one foot in the room and the other in the hallway. She glares at me.

"What, Mom?" The exhaustion causes me to slump my shoulders.

"You were talking to them." Her hair is messy, the wrinkles on her face seem deeper somehow, and the thin strap of her sundress is hanging off her shoulder, exposing half her breast. I move to correct it, but she slaps my hand away. "Were you talking about me? What do you think I am, some useless drunk, is that what you think? I just like to enjoy myself, Nina, and I don't need you talking about me behind my back, treating me like shit."

"Mom, I didn't, I wouldn't do that—"

"Shut up and listen to me." She steps out of her room and into the hall. I back against the wall behind me. Pointing toward the balcony, she snaps, "Those people think what they think of me because of you. You manipulate them, make them think you're something special, make them think there's something wrong with me. I *know*. You don't fool me."

"That's not true, Mom, and even if it was, what about you?"

"What are you saying?"

I think of the rape. I always think of it when Mom and I fight. I want to know *why*. Even though my body is trembling, my chest is tightening, and a cold sweat is crawling across my body, *I have to know*.

"You remember when I was fifteen, and I had that date, and you let him into the house, and he raped me?" I bite at my lip, dig my fingernails into my palms, my entire body shaking. "I want to know one thing. Why didn't you stop him? You were drunk in the next room, Mom. Why didn't you do something? Why'd you let him into our house?"

She turns on me, jabbing her finger, anger etched into her features. "I *trusted* you," she growls.

"Stop it!" I shout, on the verge of tears. I can't hold it back anymore. I can't handle this. I feel like I can't breathe, and my throat is tightening up, my skin clammy.

"You're a liar!" She grabs at my wrists, shoving me roughly against the wall, and even though she's small and skinny, this hurts me—not physically, but it hurts my heart and soul; it cuts me to my core.

I don't know what's happening to me now, my body quakes, I'm heaving, and I shove her back and shriek, "Don't do that, don't touch me like that!" and I'm wrapping my arms around my body as I shudder, pushing against the wall. I wish it would give, I wish the building would suck me down, down into the earth.

Panic.

I run for the kitchen. I'm wearing my pajamas—light green and white with a matching long-sleeved top—and I grab my keys, jacket, and cell phone, and suddenly I'm putting on my flip-flops, but part of me doesn't really know what I'm doing.

"Where are you going?" my mother snaps, and I pick up a hint of worry in her voice, as if she's afraid I'm going to leave and never come back.

My voice trembles. "I...I can't handle this right now, I can't do this right now, I have to leave."

"You're a goddamn coward, always running away!" She turns and stomps back to her room, where she slams the door behind her, and I rush out the front, letting it shut loudly behind me. I race to my car, not even thinking, not even knowing where I'm going.

Slam. The door shuts and I'm inside, and I'm breathing heavily, and suddenly I know I'm having a panic attack.

Calm, calm, I tell myself, but it doesn't work.

It takes a long time. I sit there in the dark, just trying to breathe, and after a while, once I finish crying, I am quiet, and everything around me is perfectly still.

Silence.

I put the key in the ignition, place the car in gear, and drive.

Chapter 9

My favorite place, Juno Beach. That's where I'm headed now, my headlights piercing the darkness as I weep. My eyes blurry, I shift into the next lane, and a car horn blares behind me before the vehicle speeds around me, and I curse myself for narrowly missing him because my tears are blinding me.

This isn't like me.

I chose to move to North Carolina because I knew I had to get away from my mother. Her sickness is poisoning me, and it's only a matter of time before I crack, before I lose it. I hit bottom tonight, and I'm slowing as I reach the intersection of Donald Ross and U.S. 1. I make a right, wiping my eyes with the back of my hand. The ocean is ahead. I need mother ocean to cleanse me, to take away this darkness.

Holiday lights glimmer from the condos, and I wish I could have set up a tree at home, but my mother wouldn't let me *make a mess in the living room*. The living room I help pay for.

I tighten my hands on the steering wheel, feeling the hurt turn to anger, and I want to scream. I think of Jenny. I could stay at her house tonight, but she still lives with her parents, and I'm too ashamed to let them see me this way. This isn't the first time I've driven off with no destination, exhausted with nowhere to sleep.

I pull over somewhere along the road near Juno Beach Ocean Park and kill the engine. New Year's Eve. There are a lot of cars here, and I see some shadows moving in the dark. I know they can't light fireworks on the beach, so I picture them making love in the sand, groaning under the dark sky, legs lifted in the air. It's a new moon, and when the headlights are off, I can't see a thing.

I consider getting out of my car and wandering down to the surf, but I'm too tired, and my body aches. Instead I pick up the phone and access my contacts, taking a chance, calling the first person I think of, and remembering how Jenny warned me to *be careful because you don't know him that well*.

It rings five times, and I consider hanging up, because he's probably at a party. Just as I start to think I should leave him be, because he hardly knows me and it's not fair to call him at a time like this, he answers.

"Nina, what's up?" He seems happy, his voice edged with laughter, and it sounds as if he's driving.

"Um...I..."

"Nina, are you okay?"

"I don't mean to bother you. You're probably headed to a party or something."

"Yeah, but that's okay. What's up?"

"I left my house, I just couldn't handle it anymore."

"Your mom?"

"Yeah." I tug at the fabric around my steering wheel, watch two shadows emerge from the beach entrance nearest my car.

"Are you okay, though?"

"Yeah, I just needed someone to talk to."

"That's all right. You can talk to me anytime. I hope you have somewhere to stay. Your friend Jenny's house?"

I think of Jenny's father, the ex-Mayor of North Palm Beach, and Jenny's mother, who always reminds me of June from *Leave it to Beaver*. I couldn't go there late at night, looking like this. Glancing at my watch, I notice it's after eleven.

"I, uh…no. I don't really have anywhere to go. I'll just stay where I am a while." As I'm talking, I'm stretching toward the back seat, tugging my pillow and blanket to the front of the car. It's not the first time I've slept in my car, and it won't be the last.

"Where are you?" Wes asks.

"Just along the ocean in Juno Beach."

"You parked on the side of the road? You're not going to sleep there, are you?"

I recline my seat and lean back against the pillow, tugging the blanket over me. "I'm exhausted. I need to sleep. I've slept here before, it's no big deal." I thought he would understand, and I realize I'm annoyed he sounds shocked.

"In your car?"

"Yeah."

"Can't you go home?"

"I know what'll happen if I go home. My mom will start on me again, unless she's passed out. But usually it takes her a while, especially if she's fired up. I'd rather wait until morning to deal with her, when she's sober. By then she'll forget everything anyway." For a moment, the line's quiet, and I start to think he hung up or my phone died. "Wes? Wes, are you there?"

"I'm here."

"Oh, I thought I lost signal or something."

"Do me a favor."

"Yeah?"

"Lock your doors."

"Of course. I always do when I spend the night here."

"I'll see you, Nina. Take care, okay?"

"I will. Thanks for listening."

"Anytime."

The line goes dead, and I'm a little upset he hadn't been able to talk longer, but I know he's on his way somewhere and he's busy. In a moment, it doesn't matter anymore, and I'm leaning back, my eyes shut as I drift into dreaming.

There's nowhere I'd rather be than at the beach.

***

I'm in a dark place, and I see myself wandering through hallways, unable to find a way out. It's an old house, decrepit, falling apart. I remember a psychic telling me once that dreaming of a house is like dreaming of your soul. The house is your spirit.

If this place was a part of me, it was dismal and broken, and I needed to fix it.

I hear someone knock at the door. I'm stepping down the stairs and they're creaking beneath my weight, and my hand is on the dusty railing. Suddenly I think there's a rapist there, at the front door, and he's going to come in and take what he wants, destroy me from the inside out, the same way I was taken when I was fifteen, naïve and unprepared. Terrified, I don't want to know who's there, I don't want to answer the door. But the knocking becomes louder, more insistent, and I blink, the room blurring and—

I open my eyes. I see darkness, the yellowish glare of a distant, weak street lamp shining down on my car. With a little effort, I remember where I am. Then I hear the knocking again, and I look over and gasp, almost scream, then clap my hand over my heart. Rubbing my eyes, I sit up, then roll down the window.

"Wes, you scared the shit out of me." I pause, looking up at him. "What are you doing here? What time is it?"

He leans on the door, peering in at me. "It's about two-thirty in the morning. Did you really think I was going to let you spend the entire night on a street somewhere?"

"It's Juno Beach, Wes, it's safe. And you drove all the way here from—"

"Never mind that." He nods ahead to a car in front of mine, its lights on. I realize it is his. "Get ready to drive and follow me, okay?"

"Where are we going?"

"A hotel, where you can get some good rest."

"A hotel at this hour? They aren't open." My voice is weak, groggy.

"I know the night manager at the Seabreeze down the street in Jupiter. I called him right after I talked to you earlier, and I booked a room and paid over the phone. It's waiting for you."

"What? Wes, you hardly—"

"Don't." He reaches in the window and takes my hand, gently caressing my fingers. "I might've just met you, but I feel like I've known you a long time, Nina. You're special to me. And I'm not going to let you sleep in your car. I have plenty of money, remember? Now, come on. I'm going to get in my car, and you follow me."

"Okay, Wes," I agree, feeling a little silly, a little childish. I want to yell, to snap at him, to say *don't tell me what to do*, but at the same time I keep picturing a soft bed, with comfortable blankets, and pillows that smell fresh and airy.

I watch him walk back to his car and climb in, and when he pulls out into the empty street, I hurriedly start my car and follow, pillow and blanket shoved onto the passenger seat.

I keep thinking, *What am I doing?* I'm going to a hotel with a man I've only known for two weeks. As I drive along the winding road, past Carlin Park, I feel as though I'm floating in the night sky, and every one of my senses is heightened, giving me the distinct impression I've done all this before.

I remembered my dream. I *had* done all this before.

When I Dream of You

The hotel. I'd been in a hotel in my dream. And here I was, repeating the past. I think of the dream where Wes was driving, and we crashed, and I think of him telling me, *It's fate, Nina*, but I still don't want to believe it.

The narrow road that leads to the hotel is lit with white lights and Christmas decorations, and I follow Wes's car into the lot across from the main entrance, parking beside him. When I climb out and lock my doors, tucking my keys and wallet into my pocket, he comes to me and wraps his arms around me, holding me close. He has something in his hand in a paper bag, and I feel it against my back.

"I'm sorry for everything you've gone through," he says.

"It's okay. I know life will get better soon," I assure him. "It's just not easy living with her."

He releases me, looking into my eyes under the bright lights in the parking lot. "I know. My parents are just distant. They don't understand me. They drink, but they never get crazy. I can't imagine what it's like living with someone who's abusive."

We start walking toward the front entrance to the hotel. I shake my head. "Mom's not abusive."

"I thought you said she screams at you when she's drunk and insults you?"

"Yeah, but she's not abusive."

"Babe, you're in denial."

I shiver, but it's not because I'm cold. He just called me *babe*, and I realize I like it. Something about this man drives me crazy.

Then I think about my mother shoving me against the wall, and the sliding glass doors, and the way she grabs me in anger and yells in my face.

"Maybe you're right," I say, my voice soft, because I'm reluctant to admit it. I want to believe it's not as bad as it sounds. I want to believe I'm exaggerating. I stop before we step inside, and I say something that's been in the back of my mind since he knocked on my window, waking me up. "I don't need rescuing, you know, so I sure hope that's not what you're doing."

Wes steps up to me and takes both my hands in his. "I'm not trying to rescue you. You're a strong woman, Nina. You're not as much of a mess as you think you are. Yes, I know what you think of yourself. I can tell. I *know* you don't need to be rescued. But I do know one thing you need, and that's a place to sleep."

He lets go of one hand, but holds my other hand in his, leading me into the lobby. His friend, the night manager, is there to give us the key. In the lobby, soft music plays, and we step into the elevator. Wes hits the button for the sixth floor, and the doors shut firmly in front of us.

If I had any misgivings about going to a hotel with him, they disappear as the elevator begins to move up, and Wes pulls me close, his arm around my waist.

***

I step out on the balcony and listen to the lapping of the ocean against the shore.

"What do you think of the room?" Wes asks.

I turn and look at the soft lighting, the small space, the immense bed taking up the majority of the suite.

"There's only one bed," I mutter, my face flushing. I glance up at him, and he slips a bottle out of the paper bag, handing it to me. As I read the label on the whiskey, my eyes downcast, I add, "But I trust you for some reason. I'm not sure why."

"You don't trust people easily, do you?" He sits down at a small desk.

"No. I didn't grow up with many positive examples of trust. My mother was never very good at giving advice, and when I followed it, I always ended up in a mess."

He nods, listening intently. "I won't be able to sleep anyway, so you take the bed." He reaches out and holds my hand again. The sensation makes my breath come quicker; my heartbeat speeds up. "You're already in your pajamas. Go ahead and relax."

I sit down on the edge of the bed, patting the mattress beside me. "Let's have a drink," I suggest, holding up the bottle.

"Are you sure?"

I nod. "It's New Year's. New beginnings. I may as well partake. Anyway, you brought it for us to share, didn't you?"

"Yes, certainly." He sits down beside me. "I thought you could use a drink after what you went through."

I sigh, shaking my head. "You thought right." I twist off the cap and lift the bottle. "Cheers." The whiskey is bitter against my tongue, and it feels good going down, filling my chest with heat that seems to wrap me up and hold me close, like a cozy blanket on a chilly winter night. I close my eyes briefly, savoring it, then hand the bottle to Wes. "You know," I begin, "I always knew when to quit. But my mother never did. I can stop drinking and not need another drink for months and months. I might *want* one, but I don't *need* one. I wonder why that is."

"You don't have the same problem your mom does." Wes takes a deep swig. "She's an alcoholic, you're not."

"Thank God. But she's always so sweet in the mornings. She makes me breakfast. Mom makes the best pancakes *ever*." I smile fondly. "I just...I know she's been through so much. But..."

"So have you."

"That's true." I think of the rape. What would Wes say if he knew?

I think of it all the time. Once, I thought I was over it, but one day I realized it was always in the back of my mind, engrained in my subconscious, and I wanted so badly to be rid of it.

Wes and I sit in silence for a while, and he hands me the bottle again. I take another deep drink, and flash back to my days in high school, when I was still seeing my therapist. I wonder how he's doing. He's probably out of jail, and I hope he's leading a normal life. I imagine he's learned his lesson. How could he not? He'd helped so many girls like me. I think about him a lot, perhaps because I wonder why someone in his position could do what he did.

He'd raped a girl my age. After everything he'd done for me.

It could have been me.

"What are you thinking about?" Wes asks as I hand him the bottle.

"Oh, nothing. Just the past."

"Live in the present, Nina. You need to let go of everything else. It's not serving you anymore. Old thoughts, old behaviors...they're no good." He takes a sip and hands the bottle back to me, then gets up to go to the bathroom. When he returns, he plops down on the other side of the bed. "Okay if I lay here? I'll be good, I promise."

I laugh, half-wishing he'd be bad instead, then I throw my legs up on the bed and lean against the headboard, a pillow behind my back.

A few long minutes pass, and I clear my throat, clutching the bottle. "Wes, can I tell you something?"

"Of course, Nina." His hands are clasped over his stomach, and he's lying on the bed under the comforter, his head on a pillow, staring up at the ceiling.

"I..." The words break inside me. I don't know how to say it. I'm so terrified of intimacy, so torn up inside. But there's a yearning I can't deny, and I don't know how to reconcile it with my fears. "Wes, I...I really need you to hold me right now."

He shifts to his side and lifts the blanket. "Come here," he says softly.

And I do.

Chapter 10

Present day, Jupiter, Florida

I speed over the bridge on Indiantown Road, and it isn't until I reach the intersection at Military Trail that I realize I'm running from him. My breath is coming quicker, my hands tightening on the steering wheel until my knuckles are white. I gasp, breathe in deep, sob uncontrollably, and each cry makes my whole body shudder as I slow down and pull over, putting my hazard lights on.

Where am I going? I don't even know. I'm directionless, and the road stretches out before me, deserted and dark. A stranger wrapped in a dirty blanket steps off a side street and crosses, and I wonder how alone they are, how lost they are.

My head falls forward and I weep, my face soaked with tears, and I keep crying until I have nothing left. Being underneath him, pressed against the mattress, his erection pulsing against my thigh, I'd squirmed like a trapped animal, and every instinct inside me reacted with run, run, run.

Panic. Those memories return full-force, and it's like I'm being raped all over again, and he's driving himself inside me, merciless, chuckling like he's watching a one-woman comedy being acted out on stage, and when he comes, he grunts and falls on top of me, and when it's over—

When it's over, I lay there, feeling used like trash, my body naked and chilled, and I whisper to myself, "That wasn't so bad."

But it was, and every time I get close to someone, I *panic*.

Just before I left the hotel, Wes had said, "You need to learn to be intimate again," and I know he's right. I remember my dreams, the word *fate* echoing in the back of my mind.

I pull my head up. All I can hear is the *tick-tick-tick* of the hazard lights as my turn signals blink, and I see the orange flashing against the dark road.

I don't even think anymore. I turn off the hazard lights and put the car in first gear, then spin around. No traffic, no one to stop me. I shoot across the intersection, then do a U-turn, speeding back toward the bridge, back toward the beach.

Minutes later, I'm heading down the narrow drive and into the lot at Seabreeze, slowing into a spot and throwing the gearshift in first again. I turn off the car, take my foot off the clutch.

There's no one at the front desk, and the soft music is still playing in the lobby. I head for the elevator and press the button for the sixth floor, anxious to get there before I change my mind again.

The hallway is silent, narrow, and every door looks the same. I walk along the carpeting toward the room, and knock sharply below the peephole. A few moments pass as I wait.

Am I doing the right thing?

Somehow I know I am.

When he answers the door, he steps aside, smiling, his eyes betraying his exhaustion. "I knew you'd come back."

"How?" When I enter, he closes the door and turns to me.

"Fate." He steps close to me, drawing me near.

"I don't believe in fate."

"How could it be anything else, Nina?" His mouth is so close to mine, and he leans in to kiss me, crushing me against his body.

As he's kissing my neck, then my shoulder, my eyelids flutter, and I say, "Please, please take it slow, I'm scared...it reminds me of..."

"I know." His voice is soft. "You don't need to explain."

He leads me to the bed and then sits down, pulling me forward. Now I'm straddling him, and he's tugging my pajama shirt over my head. I'm scared, but I feel safer not trapped beneath him, and my heart pounds as he kisses me and we taste each other. Then he takes his shirt off, presses me against him, and his skin is so warm and soft that a wave of heat passes over me, making every part of me tingle with anticipation as my nipples harden against him.

"Is this okay?" he asks, his voice husky, filled with need.

"Yes, it's okay."

He kisses me along my jawline, then down to my neck, and I arch my back when he reaches my nipples, taking one in his mouth and sucking hard until I moan softly.

"Lay down with me?" He kisses across my chest, then licks at my other nipple, taking it in his mouth as he squeezes my backside.

"Mmm." I can't form words anymore, and I'm telling myself, *Stay calm, it's okay, he won't hurt you.*

Gentle and strong, he lifts me up and places me down, my head against the pillow, then he slips off my pajama bottoms and my panties, leaving me naked and vulnerable before him. For a moment, this terrifies me, but he stops, because it's almost as if he knows, and he sits beside me, trailing his fingers along my hip and thigh, but moving slowly so as not to send me into a panic.

I look at his face, his brow furrowed, his eyes staring straight into mine. Then he tugs the comforter out from under me, covering me, and begins to unbuckle his pants. He stops.

"If you don't want—"

"I want you, Wes. Come here."

Wordlessly, he slips out of his pants and climbs under the blanket with me, drawing me close. There's still a part of me that wants to run, but when our bodies are pressed together, radiating heat, his arm tight around me as we lay side by side, I know there's nowhere else I'd rather be—here, by the ocean, in his arms.

He nuzzles my neck, and whispers, "You smell so good, Nina," and I feel his kisses, wet and hungry, trailing up along my chin until he finds my lips. He kisses me slowly at first, then more passionately, and this time I force the fear away; I won't get scared. I won't let myself run from him ever again.

I wrap my leg around him, drawing him as close as I can, wanting nothing more than to feel him inside me. I'm pulsing, wet, wanting, and I feel his hardness against me. He pulls away slightly, and I hear the rip of foil as he unwraps a condom. Then, with my body, I guide him toward me, and he kisses me harder, pressing me against the mattress as he plunges inside me.

This time I'm not afraid anymore.

I give myself up to his affection, and I moan, my fingernails digging into his back. I run my hands through his hair, so soft, and I kiss him, gentle, more tender than before, and he matches each kiss with his strokes, moving just the right way, pressing against me until I feel a rush of pleasure and I gasp.

When he comes, he lays against me, his head on my shoulder, still inside me. We're quiet for a long time, and I can feel his heart beating. We're connected, more than just physically, and it's as if I can feel our souls touching. Maybe it's my exhaustion, but I see colors around me, his aura entwined with mine, a rainbow dance that seems to go on forever, something that was meant to be, a work of art finally completed.

He lifts his head and looks into my eyes. Seeing his gaze this close to me, heavy with satisfaction, I peer through the dark brown and beyond, and it's almost as if I'm seeing images flash through my mind from countless past lives, where we were together, and we lost one another, then died and found each other again.

I kiss him, then look into his eyes, and he smiles, gently running his fingers along the curve of my jaw.

"I believe in fate now," I whisper. "I had to come back. Something *urged* me to come back. My dreams—"

"You don't have to tell me. I have the same dreams."

"You do?"

He nods, then moves to lie beside me, pulling me close. "Sleep, Nina. Sleep and awaken to face your fears. And I'll be here if you need me."

I close my eyes, my head tucked against him. The sliding glass doors to the balcony are open, and a gentle breeze blows over us. I can hear the ocean rushing, waves breaking against the shore, and it lulls me into a peaceful rest.

When the sun breaks through and shines bright light across the room, I awaken feeling different, freer—released from the shackles that bound me for years. Sleeping beside me, Wes stirs in a dream, and I wonder if he's dreaming of me.

I lay back on the pillow, my breasts bare to the chill air of morning, and I feel relaxed. Like a whole person again.

Complete.

Acknowledgements

Thank you to Tara Chevrestt for her wonderful constructive criticism. Even though I have yet to meet her, I will always value her friendship.

The sand and surf in Juno Beach and Jupiter also deserves my thanks. It is there—while staring over the ocean—that I've had my best ideas.

And here's to many more.

About the Author

Rosa Sophia is the author of two traditionally published mystery novels: "Taking 1960″ and "Check Out Time." She is a full-time editorial consultant, and has worked for publications such as The Bucks County Writer, Wild River Review, Sunshine Press, and Limitless Publishing, to name a few. She also teaches and leads workshops on writing and publishing. Addicted to writing, Rosa is working on several projects, including a non-fiction book on South Florida that blends memoir and history. With a degree in Automotive Technology, she adores writing and editing, as well as fixing cars. Rosa currently divides her time between South Florida and Pennsylvania, and enjoys running and hiking. She is a proud member of the Editorial Freelancers Association.

Facebook:
www.facebook.com/editing.by.rosa.sophia

Twitter:
https://twitter.com/rosysophia

Goodreads:
www.goodreads.com/author/show/4116872.Rosa_S
ophia

Website:
www.rosasophia.com/
www.backwordswriter.com/

Made in the USA
Middletown, DE
25 October 2014